Parents and Caregivers,

Stone Arch Readers are designed to provide enjoyable reading experiences, as well as opportunities to develop vocabulary, literacy skills, and comprehension. Here are a few ways to support your beginning reader:

- Talk with your child about the ideas addressed in the story.

- Discuss each illustration, mentioning the characters, where they are, and what they are doing.

- Read with expression, pointing to each word. You may want to read the whole story through and then revisit parts of the story to ensure that the meanings of words or phrases are understood.

- Talk about why the character did what he or she did and what your child would do in that situation.

- Help your child connect with characters and events in the story.

Remember, reading with your child should be fun, not forced. Each moment spent reading with your child is a priceless investment in his or her literacy life.

Gail Saunders-Smith, Ph.D.

Stone Arch Readers

are published by Stone Arch Books
a Capstone Imprint
1710 Roe Crest Drive
North Mankato, Minnesota 56003
www.capstonepub.com

Library of Congress Cataloging-in-Publication Data
Crow, Melinda Melton.
Rocky and Daisy get trained / by Melinda Melton Crow; illustrated by Mike Brownlow.
p. cm. — (Stone Arch readers: My two dogs)
Summary: Rocky and Daisy go to obedience school.
ISBN 978-1-4342-4161-0 (library binding)
ISBN 978-1-4342-6116-8 (paperback)
1. Dogs—Training—Juvenile fiction. [1. Dogs—Training—Fiction. 2. Dogs—Fiction.]
I. Brownlow, Michael, ill. II. Title.
PZ7.C88536Rpf 2013
813.6—dc23   2012027139

Reading Consultants:
Gail Saunders-Smith, Ph.D.
Melinda Melton Crow, M.Ed.
Laurie K. Holland, Media Specialist

Designer: Russell Griesmer

Printed in the United States of America in Stevens Point, Wisconsin
092012
006937WZS13

Rocky and Daisy
Get Trained

by Melinda Melton Crow
illustrated by Mike Brownlow

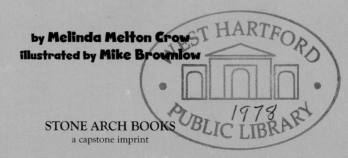

STONE ARCH BOOKS
a capstone imprint

MY TWO DOGS

I'm Owen, and these are Rocky and Daisy, my two dogs.

ROCKY LIKES:

- Chasing squirrels
- Playing with other dogs
- Chewing things
- Running with me when I ride my bike

DAISY LIKES:

- Playing ball
- Listening to stories
- Resting on the furniture
- Eating yummy treats

Owen's dogs Rocky and Daisy
were best friends. Rocky was
silly and playful. Daisy was
sweet and shy.

They were both great dogs,
but sometimes they got into
trouble.

Rocky liked to chew things.
He destroyed three TV remotes.

He ruined Mom's new shoes. He
wrecked Owen's cars and trucks.

"No, Rocky! You cannot chew everything," said Dad.

Daisy liked to rest on the furniture. She slept on Owen's bed.

She napped on the couch.

She even curled up in Mom's reading chair.

"No, Daisy! You are not allowed on the furniture," said Mom.

Owen tried to train Rocky and Daisy. He tried to teach them the rules. But it wasn't easy.

Owen needed help.

"We are going to dog school today," said Mom. "Rocky and Daisy need to learn some manners. They will learn to obey the rules," she said.

Owen and Mom took Rocky and Daisy to dog school.

"I am so excited!" shouted Rocky. He ran around and sniffed all of the dogs.

"I'm nervous," whispered
Daisy. She hid behind Mom.

The trainer's name was Miss
Grace. "Welcome to school," she
said.

Miss Grace gave all the owners a bag of dog treats. "These are rewards," she said.

"Yum! I like treats," said Rocky.

"Me too," said Daisy.

"Today, we are learning three commands. Sit, down, and stay," said Miss Grace.

Everyone stood on the red
line with their dogs on their
leashes.

First, the dogs learned to sit.

"Sit," said Owen. Rocky sat.

"Sit," said Mom. Daisy tried to sit, but the floor was slippery. She slid down onto her belly. Mom had to help her sit.

"Reward your dogs," said Miss Grace. Rocky and Daisy got a treat.

Next, the dogs learned to lie
down.

"Down," said Mom. Daisy
was good at lying down. Her
feet slid out, and she was down.

"Good girl, Daisy," said Mom.
"Here is your treat."

"Down," said Owen. Rocky
lay down.

Finally, the dogs tried the command to stay.

"Stay," said Mom. She dropped the leash and walked away.

Daisy was tired. She stayed.
In fact, she curled up and fell
asleep before Mom could give
her a treat.

"Stay," said Owen. He dropped the leash and walked away.

Rocky did not stay. He ran all over the room.

"Come on, friends," barked Rocky. The other dogs began to run and bark, too.

"Oh, goodness," said Miss Grace.
"Please practice your commands at
home. See you next week."

"Hooray, we have homework!" said Rocky. He ran around with the other dogs.

Mom and Owen took Daisy and
Rocky home. "You two still have a
lot to learn," said Owen.

"That's okay," said Daisy. "I like school."

"Especially the treats!" said Rocky.

THE END

STORY WORDS

destroyed	furniture	sniffed
wrecked	obey	especially

Total Word Count: 452

READ MORE
ROCKY AND DAISY ADVENTURES!

STONE ARCH **READERS** LEVEL 3
Rocky and Daisy Go Home

STONE ARCH **READERS** LEVEL 3
Rocky and Daisy Go Camping

STONE ARCH **READERS** LEVEL 3
Rocky and Daisy at the Park